For Thom

It was Christmas Eve eve and Indigo looked out
Of his bedroom window at the snow all about
The world was covered with glossy white waves
Engulfing everything, hiding hills, trees and caves

The moon shone so brightly through the clearest of skies
Trillions of stars, a delight for the eyes

All of a sudden the shadows and shapes changed
The tide switched direction and the lumps rearranged
From nowhere to somewhere a line of light grew
A door being opened, long forgotten... left pulled to

At first a boot stepped, then came another
Followed by one more behind the two other
A small figure squeezed through, just managing to fit
A big fluffy head with goggles on it
Wearing countless coats, jumpers, gloves and a scarf
Followed by three sloths and a long limbed giraffe

Once through the door they stared up at the night,
The stars in his goggles glittered so bright

He drew from the bag a beautiful jar
To fill with brushed snow from one lucid star
The sloths and giraffe sat down in a row
While the man pulled from his bag... a mighty great crow!

Finally, he seemed to be set for the task
He poured a warm drink from a large silver flask
He stood there still, with one hand in his pocket
From which there poked a small golden sprocket

Just at that second there appeared, to his right
A star much bigger, more colourful and bright
As it approached there followed a trail
Which formed a bright cloud on a really grand scale

The star exited left, fading into the night,
But what was to follow was a wonderful sight

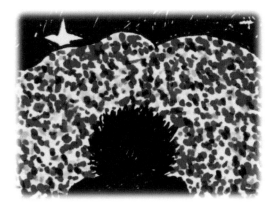

The man's gaze did not shift from the luminous fluff
He put down his hot drink and reached under his cuff
He looked at a watch and got ready to mention
The crow, sloths and giraffe jumped up to attention

Then it happened; a single snow flake floated down
From the star cloud above to the dark sleepy town

The man reached out for the jar and the sprocket
The crow flew up high as fast as a rocket
To guide the snowflake with occasional joggles
To the inside of the jar of the man with the goggles

Number one floated in with plenty of ease
Number two was directed by a mighty sloth sneeze

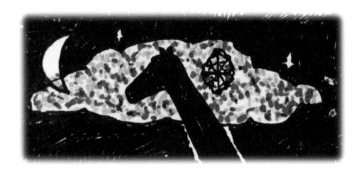

Number three skidded down the giraffe's neck
Number four made its way with no need to check

As the snow fell around them they worked as a team
Until the jar was full up as was part of their scheme

The final flake fell, drifting on to his feet
He lifted it carefully to the jar to complete
The task of collecting the luminous flakes
With no single error, falls, fails or mistakes

Now let me tell you how Indigo came to know
What this strangeness was for;
the bizarre collecting of snow

This weirdness caused Indigo to lean closer to see
The strange man with the goggles and the curiosity
He had forgotten about the warmth of his soft comfy bed
As he leaned closer to the frosty glass, he banged his head

The figure, the sloths, the giraffe and crow
Shifted their glare up, down, round to and fro
Until they settled their eyes on Indigo Brown
He ducked to the floor and let go of his frown

Seconds went by without even a creak
Until Indigo stood, to take a quick peak
They had gone, just some mess and an empty space
Some skids and imprints where they had once given
chase

A glass jar sat on the floor by a warm woolen coat
Inside the top pocket was a hand written note

The note I recall with very little missed
I will try to get it all but this is the gist

Dear Mr Galarnee, I write to you now
It is that time again, nearly Christmas somehow!
As always the children send me their wishes in a letter
But you know as I do that there is another way, better
Their dreams build up throughout the whole year
To form a unique thing beyond the atmosphere
They gather in a star that visits on Christmas Eve eve
To sprinkle the dreams of those who believe

Every snowflake is unique just like them
Their thoughts and their feelings precious like a gem

Mr Galarnee, thank you for catching them all
Thank you to your team, for easing their fall
To grant the world's wishes in bringing such joy
To every little girl and every small boy

Finally, there is, just one wish outstanding
For a boy up in the window, next to the landing
There is a boy who asked to see how wishes are made
From the point of creation to how they are paid

Please leave this jar for a boy in this town
Please grant the wish of Indigo Brown

Yours sincerely,
Father Christmas

10893848R00016

Printed in Germany
by Amazon Distribution
GmbH, Leipzig